THE CREEPER DIARIES

BOOK FIVE

CREEPER FAMILY VACATION

Also by Greyson Mann

The Creeper Diaries

The Creeper Diaries

Mob School Survivor

Creeper's Got Talent

Creepin' Through the Snow: Special Edition

New Creep at School

The Overworld Games

Secrets of an Overworld Survivor

Lost in the Jungle

When Lava Strikes

Wolves vs. Zombies

Never Say Nether

The Witch's Warning

Journey to the End

THE CREEPER DIARIES

BOOK FIVE

CREEPER FAMILY VACATION

GREYSON MANN
ILLUSTRATED BY AMANDA BRACK

Sky Pony Press
New York

THE CREEPER DIARIES: CREEPER FAMILY VACATION. Copyright © 2018 by Hollan Publishing, Inc.

Minecraft® is a registered trademark of Notch Development AB.

The Minecraft game is copyright © Mojang AB.

Sky Pony Press books may be purchased in bulk at special discounts for sales promotion, corporate gifts, fund-raising, or educational purposes. Special editions can also be created to specifications. For details, contact the Special Sales Department, Sky Pony Press, 307 West 36th Street, 11th Floor, New York, NY 10018 or info@skyhorsepublishing.com.

Sky Pony® is a registered trademark of Skyhorse Publishing, Inc.®, a Delaware corporation.

Minecraft® is a registered trademark of Notch Development AB. The Minecraft game is copyright © Mojang AB.

Visit our website at www.skyponypress.com.

10 9 8 7 6 5 4 3 2

Library of Congress Cataloging-in-Publication Data is available on file.

Special thanks to Erin L. Falligant.

Cover illustration by Amanda Brack
Cover design by Brian Peterson

Hardcover ISBN: 978-1-5107-3115-8
E-book ISBN: 978-1-5107-3117-2

Printed in the United States of America

DAY 1: SUNDAY

FAMILY. VACATION.

Those are two words I don't usually like to put together.

Don't get me wrong—I love my family and all. But hanging out with my three sisters isn't exactly my idea of a "vacation."

My oldest sister, Cate the Fashion Queen, is always moping around about some boy she is or isn't going out with. My youngest sister, Cammy the Exploding

Baby, blows herself up CONSTANTLY. The girl has zero self-control. And my Evil Twin, Chloe? Don't even get me started.

But I don't really want to hang out here at home all summer either. My buddy Sam the Slime is already getting on my nerves. I mean, I can only watch him loving up his cat Moo so many days in a row. Did I mention I'm not a huge fan of cats?

Plus, every time I show up at Sam's house, his girlfriend is there, too. I like Willow Witch and all, but sometimes a guy just wants to hang with his buddy—like the old days, when Sam and I would jump on his trampoline, just the two of us, for HOURS. That trampoline is getting pretty crowded these days, let me tell you.

So I've kind of been warming up to this vacation idea. Especially when Dad said he'd let us VOTE on where we wanted to go.

Well I didn't even have to THINK about it. If I could go anywhere in the Overworld, I'd go to the desert. Not because I like the heat—I don't. It makes me itchy. And I DEFINITELY don't like cactuses or cacti or whatever you call those poky plants that grow there.

But see, the desert is the home of my favorite rapper of ALL time: Kid Z. He lives in a desert village called Sandstone. And if I could meet him, well . . . I'd probably never ask for anything again in my whole entire creeper life.

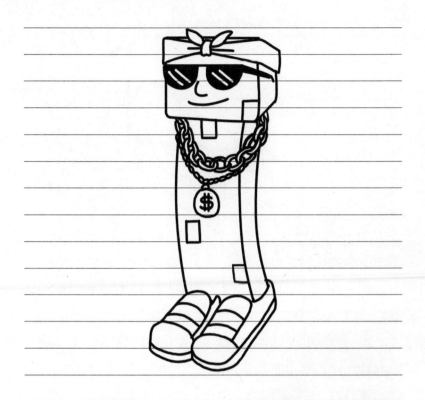

So Dad called a Creeper Family Meeting so we could all vote on our vacation ideas. And let's just say that me and my sisters didn't exactly 100% agree.

For starters, Cate said she wanted to go to the Nether. SERIOUSLY??? Who wants to lie out on a LAVA beach in the middle of SUMMER, when it's already scorching hot???

Option 1

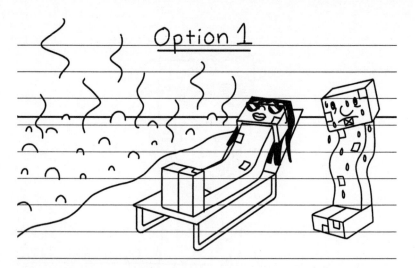

Turns out, Cate did. And all because of a BOY—her zombie pigman boyfriend, if you must know all the gory details. It's a new relationship, but if Dad has anything to say about it, it'll be the SHORTEST relationship in history too.

Chloe, on the other hand, was all about hiking in the Extreme Hills. I don't know if she REALLY wants to go there, or if she's just saying that because she knows how much I DON'T want to go there. But can you blame me? I mean, what's so fun about falling to your death in an abandoned mineshaft? Or getting bitten by a poisonous cave spider? Just saying . . . it wouldn't be my first choice.

Option 2

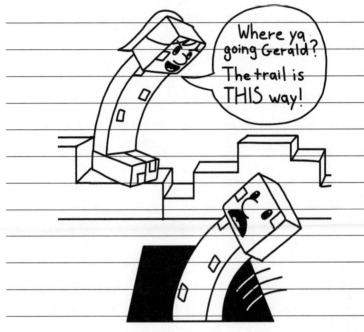

Then Mom and Dad piped up with their OWN ideas.
Well, I sure didn't see that coming.

Mom said she wanted to vacation in the jungle,
where she could find rare seeds and vines to bring
home and plant in a garden. A GARDEN? I don't
know where in the Overworld she thinks she's
going to plant THAT. I mean, she's already turned

our backyard into a BARNyard. Sock the Sheep has munched up most of the grass. And then there's that ginormous chicken coop, which is like Mom's second home.

Plus, I happen to know that the jungle is full of ocelots—big, fierce wildcats. And did I mention I'm not a fan of cats?

Dad must have been thinking the same thing, because he changed the subject so fast, Mom

didn't even know what was happening. He said HE
was hoping to get some cave camping in during our
vacation.

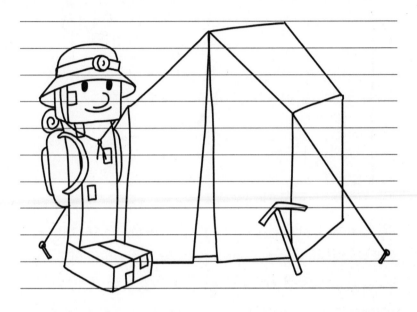

CAVE camping? Where do creepers get these crazy
ideas, anyway? I kind of wished my parents would
start talking about the garden again. But nope, Dad
was ALL about pitching a tent in a cave.

I could see it already: me waking up in my sleeping
bag with a CAVE SPIDER stuck to my face. Ah, no
thanks.

Option 4

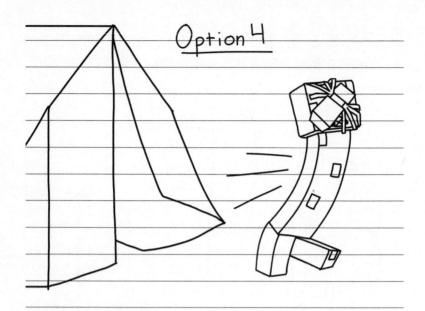

So I knew I REALLY had to push for my desert idea.
I started singing my baby sister's favorite Kid Z rap
song, because I knew she'd start singing it too.
"See?" I said. "Cammy wants to go to desert, too!"
And who's going to argue with a baby who's about
to explode with happiness at any moment?

But my other two sisters were ready for battle too.
Cate was wearing a T-shirt that said "Nether or
BUST." And Chloe pretty much busted right there on
the spot—or BURST, anyway. She said if she didn't get
to go to the Extreme Hills, she'd be so disappointed

she'd keep blowing herself up (as if that's any different from any OTHER day around here).

I could tell Dad was bummed that none of us were going for his cave camping idea. (As IF.) But then he got all excited and said he'd just had the BEST idea ever. Instead of vacationing for two weeks and only seeing a part of the Overworld, he said we should go for FOUR weeks and see LOTS of things.

"We'll ride the rails across the Overworld!" he said. "Across the plains! Through the jungle! Over the Extreme Hills! Down to the desert! We'll see it all! I mean, EXCEPT for the Nether. It's way too hot this time of year."

Cate crumpled when she heard that. I kind of felt bad for her, but I felt pretty great for myself— because I was going to the DESERT. I was going to meet Kid Z! FINALLY!

We're leaving on Tuesday, so now I'm in my room packing. Dad said we can only bring a few things. Well that sent Cate into another funk, because the girl doesn't travel lightly. She needs her WIGS, she said. Her MAKEUP! Her SKINS!

I'm not worried about packing, because I only need ONE thing—this journal. By the time I meet Kid Z, I'll have written the best rap song of all time in this trusty journal.

I AM worried about a few other things though. Like . . . How am I going to survive four weeks in a tiny minecart with my family? Sometimes our HOUSE isn't even big enough for the six of us.

And . . . will my pet squid Sticky be okay? Sam offered to watch him, which I appreciate. But Sam isn't always the most responsible slime. What if Sticky gets loose in the swamp?

And . . . what am I going to EAT for the next month? See, I'm really a roasted meat and potatoes kind of kid. But Mom says she can only pack so much food. She says we might have to "live off the land."

I gotta say, I'm not loving the sound of that. It didn't help when Dad said he'd bring his fishing pole.

I mean, I like smoked salmon, but what are the
chances of Dad catching salmon everywhere we go?
I'm going to end up eating poisonous pufferfish if I
don't plan this whole thing right.

But my biggest worry? Well, let's face it. That
would be . . . SURVIVAL. Am I gonna make it out
of this vacation alive? I mean, I like to think I'm a

brave kind of creeper. But who knows what kinds of critters we're going to run into out there in the wild?

Chloe's already saying things to freak me out, like "Bet you can't wait to meet a few ocelots in the jungle, Gerald," and "Don't you just LOVE sleeping with cave spiders?" That girl really knows how to light my fuse.

HA HA HA

So it's time to come up with a serious survival plan, something like this:

30-Day Survival Plan

- I gnore Chloe - do NOT let her freak me out.
- Sneak NORMAL food in my backpack.
- Write the BEST rap song ever while we're riding the rails.
- Stay alive long enough to meet Kid Z.

I'm kind of kidding about that last one, but not TOTALLY. I mean, bad things happen, right?

That's why a creeper has to have a plan. And besides, if I get to meet Kid Z at the end of this 30-day trip, I'll make it. I can survive ANYTHING.

DAY 3: TUESDAY

So we've been riding the rails for what feels like ages. I want to ask Dad if we're almost there, but I'm trying to keep my mouth shut.

See, the last two times I asked, Mom shot me The Look. (You know the one.) And it's WAY too early in the trip to get on Mom's bad side.

Things started out okay. Dad filled up the furnace cart with charcoal and tossed our luggage into the chest cart. He was all happy and whistling, maybe because everything actually fit.

But then it was time to choose our seats. At least I THOUGHT we'd get to choose our seats. But see, Mom and Dad already had that all worked out.

Dad said _he and Mom_ would ride in front with Cammy. So I figured Cate and Chloe could take the middle cart, and I'd take the back. If you ask me, I was being _pretty_ generous. Everyone knows that the front carts are the smoothest ride and the back carts are the jerkiest.

But Dad said that Chloe would be sharing the middle cart with ME—that Cate could have the back cart all to herself! I guess he was trying to get back on Cate's good side, because she was still moping about not going to the Nether—and because Dad only let her bring one wig along. Sometimes parents are SO unfair.

Anyway, as soon as we hit the powered rail and took off toward the jungle, Chloe and I started fighting. She thought I was hogging the seat, but how's a creeper supposed to write in his journal when he's all squished up against the side of the cart?

Then Dad started singing this song: "99 Bottles of Potion on the Wall." It was kind of dumb, but kind of catchy too. Mom started singing, and Chloe joined in, and even Baby Cammy bopped her head to the beat. Before I knew it, that song was coming out of MY mouth.

If anyone from Mob Middle School had seen us flying down the rails singing that song, I would have died of mortification. But the only critters we passed on the plains were cows and horses, their eyes glowing in the moonlight. And I think they actually kind of liked our singing.

Then Mom spotted something along the side of the rails. "Stop!" she hollered at Dad. "Stop the cart! I saw some sunflowers!"

I'd almost forgotten about Mom's plan to collect seeds. I guess Dad had too, because he just hollered back in a jolly voice, "We're not stopping! Not till morning!" Then he started singing again.

But Mom didn't. So that's when I knew we were in for it. We were still heading north, but our trip had just taken a turn to the south.

Next thing you know, Cate squealed. She sounded like a ghast in the Nether—I'm not even kidding.

I spun around in my seat just in time to see her wig fly off her head. It attacked a signpost along the railway and then tumbled off into the darkness.

"Stop the cart!" she screamed.

Dad sung back, "We're not stopping!"

So we kept going. But if Cate was mopey before, she was MAD now. Her bald green forehead was all scrunched up, her sunglasses had slid down to the end of her nose, and she was shooting arrows at the back of Dad's head with her eyes.

Everything got really quiet after that. Perfect! I started working on my rap song. I was going to add a bunch of verses—like all the things my dad WOULDN'T stop the cart for. A herd of zombie pigmen. Wither skeletons. The Ender Dragon himself!

That was right about the time the railway got curvy, and I discovered the one thing Dad WOULD stop for.

See, I might have had a few too many roasted pork chops for dinner. I guess when Mom said we would be "living off the land," I got scared. I loaded up my plate, stuffed a bunch of chops in my mouth, and even threw some leftovers into my backpack.

But now, every time we went around a curve, those pork chops slid around in my stomach.

Maybe it was because I was trying to write in my journal in the dark. Or maybe I was wrong about the last cart being the jerkiest. Either way, I told Dad I was going to be sick.

He took one look at my face, which was probably even greener than normal, and guess what?

He stopped the cart. A few seconds too late.

Anyway, we're taking a break by the side of the railway now. There's a cow staring at me, which reminds me of how my pet squid Sticky stares at me from inside his aquarium. Just thinking about

Sticky makes me homesick, and homesick plus cart-sick equals REALLY sick. So I'm gonna have to stop thinking about Sticky now.

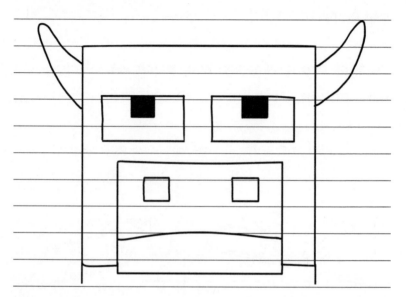

The good news is, Chloe says I can have the middle cart all to myself for a while. She's going to ride with Cate, thank you very much.

The bad news is, Mom says I can't write in my journal anymore while the cart is moving. So . . . a long trip just got way longer.

Wish me luck.

DAY 4: WEDNESDAY MORNING

Did I mention that Dad's not big on asking for directions?

We rode the rails all night toward Creeperville. That's where Dad said we'd stop in the morning for some food and a good day's sleep. Except we didn't end up in Creeperville. Nope. There's not a single creeper in this village—I mean, except for my family. But there are a whole lot of humans.

Yup, you heard me right. HUMANS. So Dad must have missed a curve in the track or something, but he'll NEVER admit that.

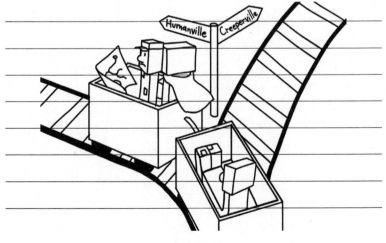

Dad's not a fan of humans, especially after a miner named Steve broke Cate's heart. But Dad is determined to make this the best creeper family vacation EVER, I can tell. He plastered a smile on his face and crept up to the first human he saw, as if they were besties or something. And he asked where some creepers could get some good food and a place to sleep around here.

For some reason, that human took one look at Dad and ran the other way. I mean, Dad DOES look kind of scary when he's fake-smiling, but still . . .

Mom tried talking with this lady in a white robe, but that was a no-go, too. She slammed the door right in Mom's face. RUDE!

Even Cate got all flirty when she saw a young farmer guy pushing an apple cart. Then she caught her reflection in a shop window and must have remembered she wasn't wearing her wig, because she turned three shades of green and started slinking behind Mom.

Anyway, I'm the one who saved the day. I only did what any smart creeper would do—I followed my nose. And it led me to the back of this butcher shop, where this guy in a white apron was cooking meat in a charcoal furnace. I didn't actually SEE the meat, but I knew it was there. Oh, yeah—I'd know the smell of pork chops ANYWHERE.

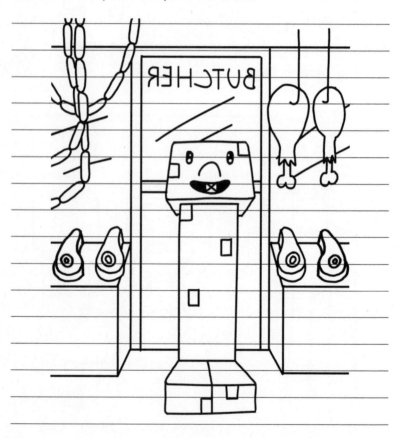

I must have surprised the butcher, because his eyes got real wide. But when I asked if we could buy a pork chop dinner from him, he was all like "Um . . . sure! Whatever you want!" He said we didn't even have to PAY for it—that we could just take it and go. RIGHT AWAY. How nice is that?

The pork chops weren't burnt to a crisp the way I like them, and the potatoes were kind of raw and crunchy, but hey . . . creepers on the road can't be too picky, right?

Since the butcher was so nice to us, Dad said we should ask him for a place to stay, too. But by the time we got back to the butcher shop, it was all closed up and dark. Dad banged on the door for a while, and Chloe started getting all hissy and impatient.

The butcher must have heard her hissing, because he finally opened the door. And he said we could sleep in his house next door as long as we didn't blow anything up. He was looking right at Chloe when he said that, and he looked kind of scared. Who can blame him? Chloe is pretty much a block of TNT with legs.

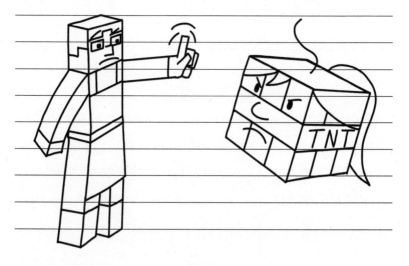

34

The butcher only has one bed, so Mom and Cate
get that. The rest of us are spread out on the floor
with blankets. And I can't sleep a wink, because rap
songs are flowing through my head like hot lava . . .

Humans running in the night
In robes of brown and black and white
Being rude and slamming doors
Making creeps sleep on the floor...

Pork chop, why you gotta be so raw?
Creepers don't like chops like THIS.
Pork chop, why you gotta be so raw?
We like you black-burned to a CRISP.

How's a creep supposed to sleep
His sis is snoring like a pig,
He's tried to count a trillion sheep,
But Chloe's mouth is oh so BIG...

So Chloe just woke up and says my torch is BLINDING her and that it's already really bright in this house and would I please just put out my torch and go to sleep.

Well, you know what happens if Chloe doesn't get her way. Yup. BOOM. And we don't want the butcher kicking us out, so . . . gotta go. I'll write more tonight.

Zzz . . .

DAY 3: WEDNESDAY NIGHT

So our new butcher friend was super helpful when we got up tonight. When Dad asked where we could get some coal for our minecart, he pointed us toward the blacksmith shop. And when Mom asked where we could get a map, he pointed her toward the library. Then he hurried us right out the door before we could even thank him for being so nice!

Dad wasn't crazy about the idea of getting a map. "It'll cost lots of emeralds," he reminded Mom. But she kept walking toward that library.

"I know where we're going," he said. "I'll just follow the signs!" She didn't even respond to that.

But when Mom knocked on the door to the library, guess who answered? That rude woman in the white robes. And the door slammed shut before Mom could even introduce herself. SHEESH.

I almost NEVER see my mom blow up, but she was seconds away from a full-on explosion. She scooped up Cammy and marched down the stairs, and she didn't stop until we'd made it all the way back to the minecart.

So I guess we're leaving Humanville. Pronto.

Mom and Dad are arguing now because during Mom's dramatic exit out of town, we forgot to stop at the blacksmith for coal. Dad says we'll be fine—we have enough coal to make it to the jungle. He's already humming "99 Bottles of Potion on the Wall," eager to hit the road.

Mom doesn't look so sure. But she doesn't look like she wants to go back into Humanville anytime soon, either. So now we're piled into our carts, and Dad is firing up the furnace.

I'm ALMOST looking forward to getting to the jungle. At least I was. But Chloe is trying to freak me out.

I'd turn around and hiss at her, but Mom's not in the mood for any cart fights. So I'm just going to have to plan a different sort of revenge . . .

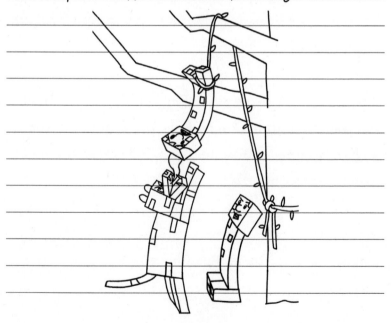

DAY 5: THURSDAY

So . . . I think it's time to pull out my 30-Day Survival Plan and dust it off. Because I barely survived day ONE in the jungle. Seriously.

It started out fine and dandy, the way daymares usually do. As we rode toward the jungle, the trees got all tall and leafy. It was actually kind of pretty.

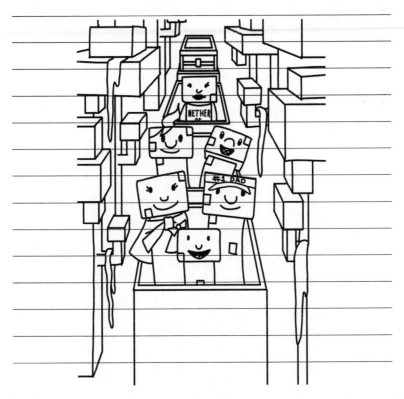

Mom was like, "The vines! The cocoa pods!" Dad was like, "Twenty-two bottles of hot cocoa on the wall . . ." And Chloe was like, "The ocelots are going to EAT YOU UP, Gerald. Better say your goodbyes now."

So when we reached the railway stop, I didn't want to get out of the cart. I wanted to keep right on going.

Then our guide showed up—this zombie dude—and he said he was going to lead us to our tree house.

Our WHAT now? You'd think Dad might have mentioned something about a TREE house. Creepers aren't exactly known for their tree-climbing skills.

But whatever. I just wanted to get to that tree house FAST, because ocelots were probably lurking all around us.

Unfortunately, our zombie guide was slower than mud. I practically had to PUSH him down the trail.

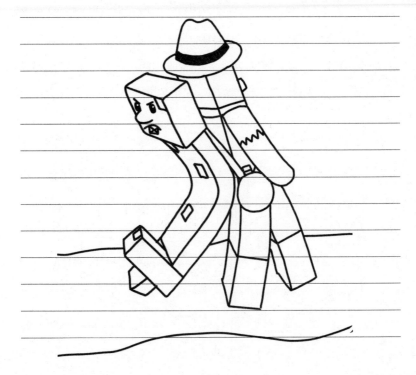

Then he stopped for a break! He sat right down on this log and offered us a snack, which turned out to be chunks of rotten flesh—the kind my sort-of pal Ziggy Zombie eats for lunch at school.

Yeah, no thanks. I took a pass on that one. And I stared at the guide until he finally stood up, wiped off his fleshy fingers, and staggered slowly toward the trail again. SHEESH. Did no one else fear for their lives around here?

I finally saw the tree house up ahead, and I almost broke into a jog. But the zombie held out his arm and said to wait up, because he had some advice for us.

First, he told us which ponds to fish in. I guess some ponds are stocked with salmon and others are full of poisonous pufferfish. Okay, good to know.

Then our guide told us to—wait for it—watch out for OCELOTS. Chloe snickered at me, but I ignored her. Because our guide was still talking.

He said that if an ocelot got too close, we could throw a piece of fish at it and then run away. A few people have even TAMED ocelots with fish, said the guide, but he wouldn't recommend that.

Then he sniffed the air and asked which one of us was wearing perfume. Well, DUH. We all stared at Cate, who pretty much always reeks of the stuff. Her latest scent is glistering melon, which at least smells better than the gunpowder she usually wears.

But the guide said Cate would want to wash off her perfume right away, because it would probably attract—you guessed it—ocelots.

I took a GIANT step away from Cate when I heard that, just in case an ocelot was about to pounce. If that happened, she was on her own. I mean, I might holler for *help* or something, but I was NOT going to fight an ocelot to protect my stinky sister.

When the sun came up, our zombie guide disappeared. And I somehow made it up the vine ladder into the tree house. In fact, I'm pretty sure I was the FIRST one up.

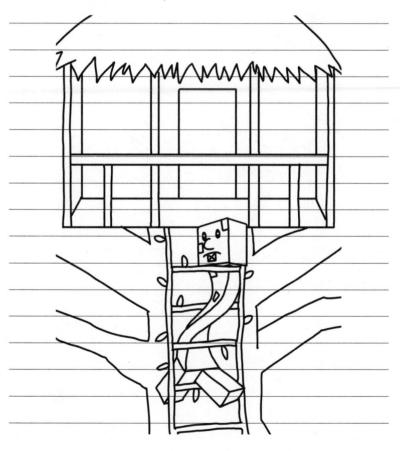

Everyone else is getting ready for bed, but I'm writing. And Mom is snipping some vine to take home for her garden.

Dad just cracked some joke about making sure Mom doesn't snip the vine off our ladder, because we might need that when we wake up tonight. But as far as I'm concerned, Mom can snip that whole ladder to pieces.

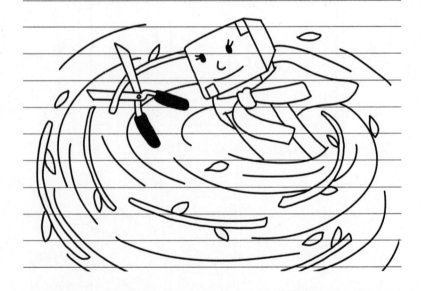

Because if there are ocelots out there, I'm never going back down.

DAY 6: FRIDAY

I went back down the ladder last night. I HAD to. I blame it on Mom, who tricked me. And on Sam, who loves hot cocoa.

See, Dad got up at the crack of dusk to go fishing. He says that's when the fish are biting. He invited me to go too, but I faked sleep. A creeper's gotta do what a creeper's gotta do, right?

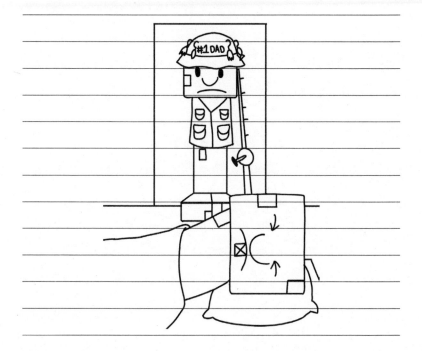

So Chloe went fishing with Dad. But when Mom said she and Cammy were heading out to look for cocoa beans, I perked right up.

"Cocoa?" I asked. "As in HOT cocoa?"

My buddy Sam LOVES hot cocoa. We sometimes go to the Creeper Café and get super deluxe hot chocolates with whipped cream and sprinkles. I don't love them as much as Sam does, but out here in the jungle, I wasn't sure where my next meal was coming from. So when Mom said that hot chocolate WAS made from cocoa beans, I slid down that ladder after her.

But when we found cocoa beans hanging from a tree, they did NOT look like hot chocolate.

For one thing, they were hard. I know this because one fell from a branch and bounced right off my head.

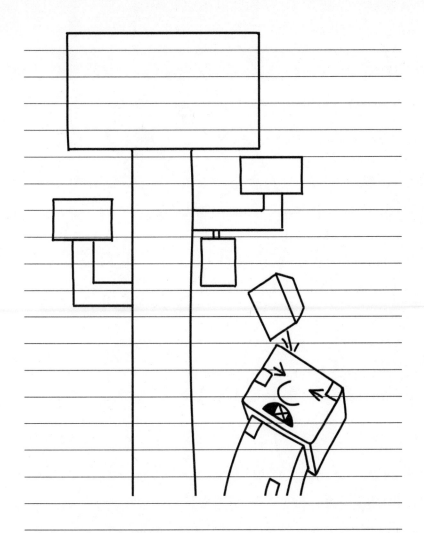

And here's another thing: they're empty. I shook
one, hoping there was hot cocoa inside. But no. It
sounded as hollow as my stomach was starting to
feel.

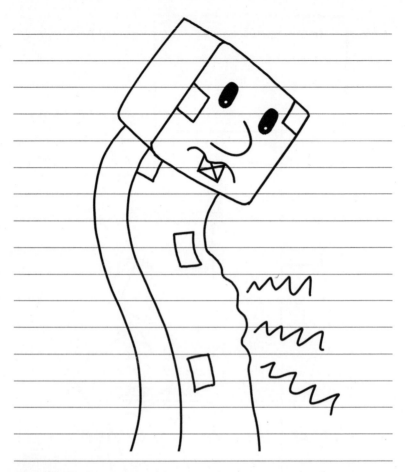

So there'd be no hot chocolate for me today.

But Mom seemed pretty happy as she gathered cocoa beans to take home for her garden. I decided to bring one home to Sam, too—like a souvenir. I was actually starting to miss that jolly green guy.

When I asked Mom if I could send Sam a postcard, she said no—that there weren't exactly post offices out here in the jungle.

But that doesn't mean I can't write to Sam. Here's what I've got so far:

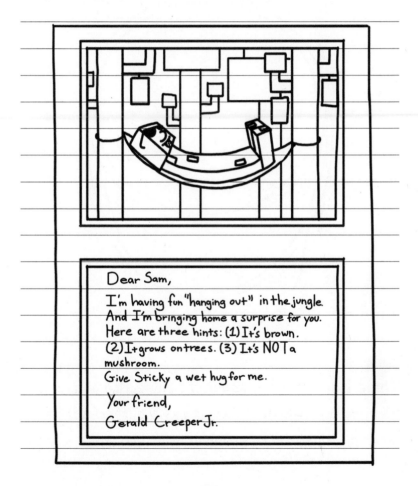

Dear Sam,

I'm having fun "hanging out" in the jungle. And ~~I'm bringing~~ home a surprise for you. Here are three hints: (1) It's brown. (2) It grows on trees. (3) It's NOT a mushroom.

Give Sticky a wet hug for me.

Your friend,
~~Gerald Creeper Jr.~~

DAY 7: SATURDAY

Let's just say that Dad did NOT catch salmon for dinner last night. He came back in the middle of the night with a seriously empty bucket.

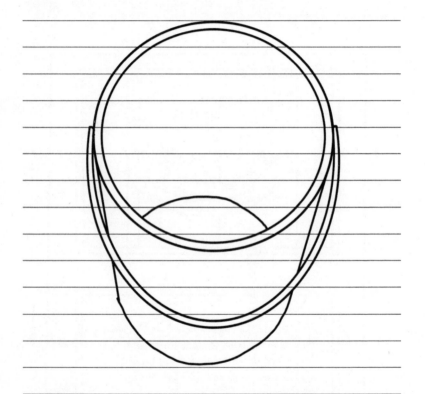

Chloe kept bragging about the huge fish SHE caught. But it turned out, it was a pufferfish. So what did she want, a trophy or something?

So Mom pulled out her snacks from home, but I gotta say, we were getting down to the crumbs now. The bread had mold on it (GROSS), so I let my sisters fight over that. I went for the carrots and apples instead. And afterward, when no one was looking, I MIGHT have snuck some roasted pork chop leftovers from my backpack.

They were kind of shriveled up and stinky. But I'd take stinky, shriveled pork chops over moldy bread any day.

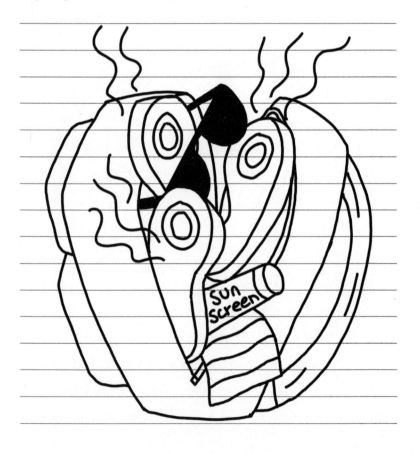

Later, when everyone else was sleeping, my stomach kept me awake. We kind of had a whole conversation, my hungry stomach and me. It wanted me to eat the rest of the pork chops from my backpack. I wanted to save some for later, just in case things got REALLY desperate out here in the jungle.

My stomach won out.

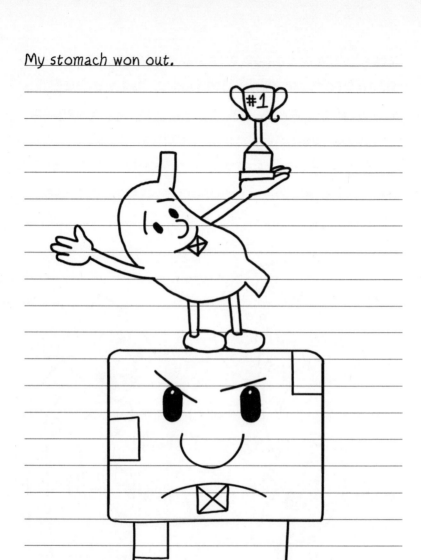

But just as I was unzipping my backpack, Dad sat up,
rubbed his eyes, and said, "FISHING time!"

When *he* saw I was awake, he was all like, "Oh good—you're up. You can come with me tonight, Gerald!"

In *his* excitement, Dad pretty much woke up the whole family. Chloe got dressed for fishing. Mom and Cammy got ready for bean-collecting or vine-snipping or whatever.

But I just yawned and said, "I'm good here." I couldn't wait for everyone to leave so I could scarf down the last of my pork chop leftovers in peace.

Then Cate said SHE was going to stay in the tree house too. She opened her chest and pulled out her makeup, and then she sprayed herself with glistering melon perfume. Except she missed her own neck—and hit ME right in the FACE.

Mom scolded her, but it was too late. Cate said she forgot about the "no perfume" rule. Yeah, RIGHT.

Well, I wasn't going to sit up here in the tree house waiting to get eaten by an ocelot who wanted glistering melon for dinner. Nope, I needed to take a bath. Pronto.

So I slid down the vine ladder and hightailed it to
the nearest pond.

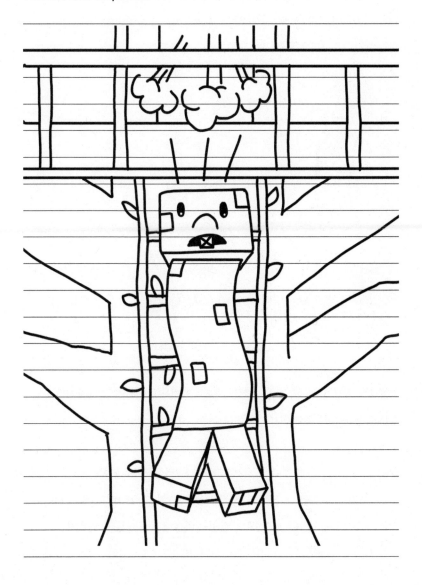

Dad ran along beside me, happy as could be. He must have thought I was excited about fishing or something. But when we got to the pond, I dove headfirst into the water.

I held my breath as long as I could, and then I finally swam to shore.

Dad was sitting on a rock with his fishing pole. Chloe was too. When she cast her line, I swear she aimed for my head. So when I walked past her, I might have shaken off some water in her direction.

That's when Dad got a bite on his line. "It's a big one!" he yelled. "Stand back!"

He fought that thing hard, I gotta say. But Dad's "big one" turned out to be a leafy vine. A really LONG leafy vine. Poor Dad.

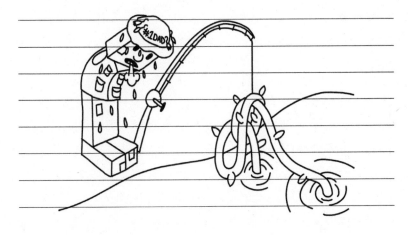

I cast my line, too. Then I waited. But I don't really get the whole fishing thing. I mean, most of the time, you're just watching your pole, and NOTHING happens. Then when it does, it's usually a gross pufferfish.

Or a vine. Or someone else's line all tangled up in yours. (Thanks, Chloe.)

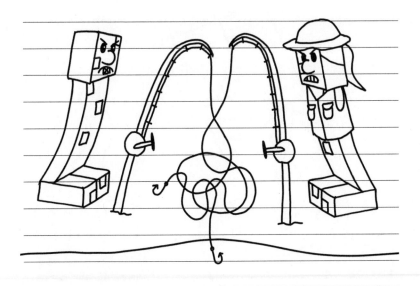

Turns out, the only one of us who caught a decent fish was Chloe. I pointed out right away that it was a CLOWNfish, not salmon. Everyone knows that clownfish don't taste very good.

But the truth was, I was drooling. You know how when you're really hungry, just THINKING about food makes your mouth fill up with saliva?

All I could think about was that clownfish smoking over charcoal.

I wiped the drool off my chin before Chloe could see it. I couldn't WAIT to get back to the tree house so Mom could cook up that fish.

But over our campfire, the clown fish shrunk right before my eyes. It got smaller and smaller and smaller. And by the time it was done cooking, it was about the size of Cammy's foot.

Then Mom cut it up into six pieces. Six TINY pieces.

I didn't even chew mine. I just swallowed it whole.
Then I had to listen to Chloe chew hers slowly, right
next to me, making lots of smacking noises too. That
creeper is SO annoying.

I pretended like I didn't want any more of Chloe's
clown fish. I grabbed a hunk of moldy bread and
tore into it, pretending to enjoy every bite.
Pretending like I DIDN'T want to throw up.

So now I'm wondering: Are we going to starve out here? Do I have enough pork chop leftovers in my backpack to get through the night? Is there a restaurant around here that I don't know about? Or (GASP) . . . is our zombie guide going to show up and save us with his rotten flesh snacks?

GROSS.

Mom busted out the last of our carrots and apples, and Dad promised that he'd catch us some salmon tomorrow. But I'm not holding my breath.

Well, maybe I'm holding my breath a LITTLE. Because I gotta say, the pork chops in my backpack are really starting to stink.

DAY 8: SUNDAY

I had the SCARIEST daymare while I was sleeping today. Except when I woke up, I realized it WASN'T a daymare. It actually HAPPENED.

I'm still shaking like a slime on caffeine—the way Sam gets the jitters from too much hot chocolate. I can't stop!

Here's how it all went down:

I was sound asleep, dreaming about an ocelot. I could hear it growling. It was getting closer and closer. It crouched low, ready to attack. And then it SPRANG at me!

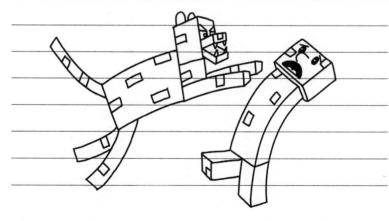

I'm not gonna lie, I screamed.

And then that ocelot was on top of me. Except it wasn't the ocelot—it was Chloe trying to wake me up. And Mom was shushing me, telling me to be quiet because there was a critter outside.

Well I sure got quiet then—I mean, except for the THUD, THUD, THUD of my heart pounding in my ears. And then I heard it again. The GROWL of an ocelot.

Dad looked down the tree house ladder and whispered the words I DREADED. "It's an ocelot."

I about dropped dead right there on the spot, but Dad was super calm. He said the ocelot was sniffing up at the tree, like it could smell food. "Do we have any food in here?" he asked.

Everyone shook their heads. Everyone except ME.

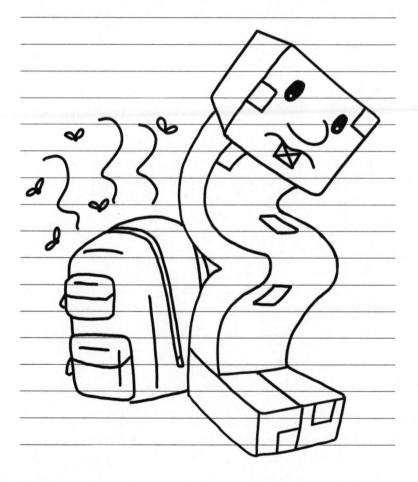

Because I DID have food up here. And my secret stash of pork chops was about to get us all killed.

Well, I sprang into action. Super Gerald flung that backpack of meat as far out the tree house door as he could. I was *pretty proud* of that fling, especially when I *heard* the backpack hit the ground a LONG ways away. Phew!

Then we all waited, but we didn't hear any more growling. Everyone else went back to sleep, but not me. No sirree. I've pretty much been awake since then. Because I just remembered something about cats, something I learned while hanging out with Sam and his cat Moo.

Cats can climb TREES.

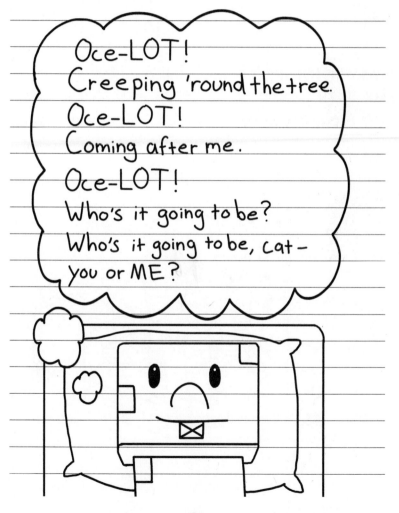

Oce-LOT!
Creeping 'round the tree.
Oce-LOT!
Coming after me.
Oce-LOT!
Who's it going to be?
Who's it going to be, cat—you or ME?

DAY 9: MONDAY

You'll be relieved to know that I'm still alive. Yup, I made it through the day yesterday and all night, too—SOMEHOW. But I had a few close calls, let me tell you.

When my family woke up last night, they pretty much acted like nothing had happened. As if there WASN'T a fierce animal prowling below our tree house. As if there weren't a gazillion more of those critters out there in the jungle right now!

Dad wanted to fish, as usual. And Mom made me go with him, because she wanted us to watch Cammy while she climbed a few jungle trees looking for more cocoa beans.

I have to say, part of me was kind of curious to climb down that tree and look for my backpack. Would it be torn to smithereens? But the other part of me wanted to pull my sleeping bag over my head and just hide out. Like for the rest of my life.

So I told Mom that maybe CATE could watch Cammy. Because what else was my older sister going to

do? Hang out in the tree house babysitting her
MAKEUP?

Mom started hissing, which is never a good sign.
Then she said something like "Go watch your sister,
Gerald, or we might not be taking any more family
trips during your lifetime, mister."

Well, I slid right down that ladder before she blew.
Mom's really getting in touch with her wild side out
here in the jungle. And I'm not exactly loving it.

On the way to the pond, I kept my eyes glued to the ground, looking for my backpack—I mean, except for every few seconds when I checked behind me, hoping there wasn't a four-legged feline on my trail.

We made it to the pond alive, with no backpack sightings. Chloe caught a clownfish INSTANTLY, but I didn't complain this time. If Clownfish Chloe was the creeper in the family who saved us all from starving, I'd be the first one to thank her.

Dad fished, too, while I watched Cammy. There sure are a lot of ways a baby creeper can get in trouble in the jungle. I mean, not only could she get eaten by an ocelot,

but she could wander off and get lost!

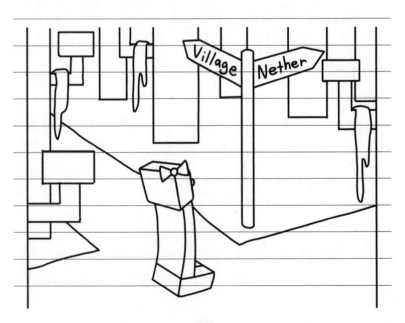

Or get beamed in the head by a cocoa bean!

Or eat a poisonous pufferfish!

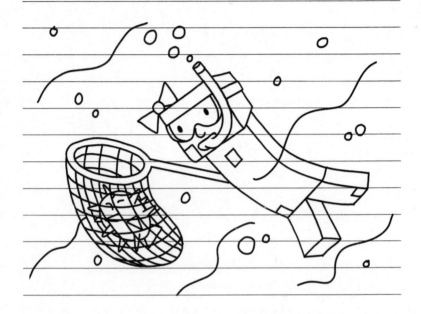

Babysitting Cammy was going to be a big job. If Mom hadn't gone all Jungle Creeper on me back there in the tree house, I would have asked for some emeralds for all this hard work.

Then Dad started complaining that his bucket was empty—that he wasn't catching anything. I tried to make him feel better. I joked, "Holy buckets, Dad. Maybe there's a hole in your bucket!"

But *he* didn't exactly fall all over *himself* laughing.

When *he* told *me* to take a turn fishing, I didn't say no. I was *happy* for an excuse to hand over my baby sister for a while.

And I'm not exaggerating here—the second I cast my line, I got a bite. Something tugged on that line, and I knew right away it was a big one.

So I jumped up and yanked on that line. And when I reeled in the fish, you'll never believe it. I caught our very first SALMON!

It was pink. It was perfect. It was BEAUTIFUL. I could

have eaten that fish raw, I swear. Except it turns
out, something else wanted to eat it too.

When I heard growling, I almost fainted on the
spot. But someone had to protect our family. So I
did what our zombie guide told us to do: I threw a
piece of fish at the cat, and I RAN.

Except it was more like the WHOLE fish. And I
didn't just run—I sprinted. For my life. Right up the
nearest jungle tree.

From the top of that tree, I watched everything
that happened next. It was like a slow-motion scene
in a movie, and I'm not even kidding.

The ocelot ate the fish, but then it wanted MORE. It crept toward Chloe and her clownfish. And she and Dad just sat there with their MOUTHS hanging open. "Run!" I wanted to scream at my family. "Save yourselves!"

But I couldn't eek out a single word. Instead, I squeezed my eyes shut and hoped for the best. I mean, maybe I was dreaming. Maybe we were all still sleeping snugly in the tree house, and this whole thing was a giant daymare.

I counted to three, and then I opened my eyes.

You'll never in a gazillion years guess what I saw.

CAMMY was feeding that ocelot another fish. And then another. The cat was right next to her now. I was SURE it was going to swallow my baby sister whole.

But it didn't. Instead, it did the strangest thing.

It licked her, and then it sat down on its rump. Like a tamed DOG.

Cammy laughed out loud and kissed the cat's head. Was it PURRING now? I could hear the thing from way up here!

Well, Dad started laughing then, too, and hollering something about how my baby sister had just tamed her first ocelot. "Get down here, son!" he called up to me.

Your sister just saved the day!

My SISTER saved the day? Had Dad not SEEN how I'd sacrificed my own fish to save the family? And how

I'd climbed this tree just to make sure that one of us survived to tell the story?

Well all the way home, I had to hear about how ONE of my sisters was the best at fishing and how my OTHER sister could tame wild animals. And by the time we got to the tree house, I realized that something had followed us there . . .

That's right—Cammy's new "pet" was now glued to her side. GREAT. Maybe it adored Cammy, but that cat still looked at me as if it wanted me for a snack. It hissed at me, and I hissed right back.

Even Dad seemed worried. "We can't take the cat with us to the Extreme Hills," he told Cammy.

When she scrunched up her face like she was going to blow, he said, "But you can play with it for one more day, till we leave. Okay, sweetie?"

"OKAY, sweetie?" REALLY, Dad? Let me just say that there is NOTHING okay about letting your baby daughter play with an ocelot.

So I don't know. The Extreme Hills are starting to look pretty good right about now. Sure, there might be cave spiders. And bats. And steep cliffs. And raging waters.

But there's one thing you WON'T find in the Extreme Hills.

CATS.

DAY 10: TUESDAY

So Cammy set the record last night for most explosions in a row—FIVE, to be exact. I'm still shaking gunpowder out of my sleeping bag.

I guess she still wants Fish to go with us to the Extreme Hills, but Mom and Dad say that's a no-go.

Yup, Cammy named her new cat "Fish." Big surprise there. This is also the girl who named our pet sheep "Sock."

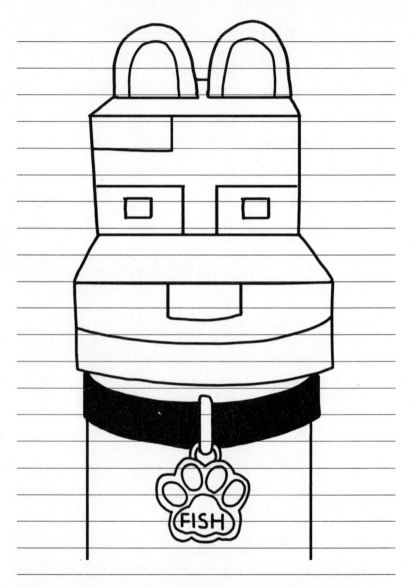

When she wouldn't stop blowing up, Mom and Dad
pulled a classic parenting trick. They told Cammy

that Fish might be waiting for us when we get back home from our trip. WINK, WINK.

Yup, they lied. Right to her face. At least it had BETTER be a lie. Because I'm not living with a cat. I'll run away and join the creeper circus first. Just saying . . .

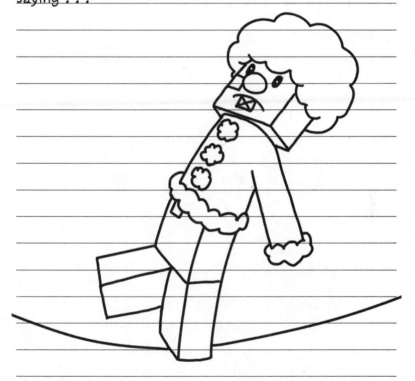

After we left Fish with our zombie guide, we waved goodbye (and good riddance). Then we loaded into our minecarts, and pretty soon, we were zooming up to the hills.

And I DO mean UP. If I weren't wearing my seatbelt, I'd probably be sitting in Cate's lap by now. Dad stopped singing for once, and Mom hung on to Cammy for dear life.

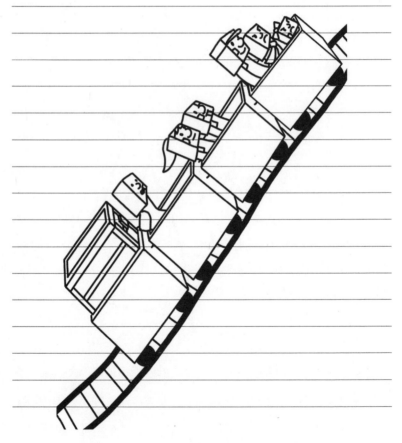

When we came to a crossroads, I read the sign out loud: "Extreme Hills ahead." Someone had painted something else on the sign in bright red, and as we inched closer, I could just make it out: "Turn back NOW!"

Well that sent a shiver down my creeper spine. And right away, the only thing I wanted to do was—yup, you guessed it—TURN BACK.

Instead, I pulled out my journal (making sure Mom didn't see me reading in the cart) and reviewed my 30-Day Plan.

30-Day Survival Plan

- I gnore Chloe - do NOT let her freak me out. (So far, so good.)
- ~~Sneak NORMAL food in my backpack.~~ (Well, THAT was a bust.)
- Write the BEST rap song ever while we're riding the rails. (Still working on it...)
- Stay alive long enough to meet Kid Z. (BINGO)

Now I remember WHY I'm doing all this—to meet Kid Z!

I'd do ANYTHING to meet Kid Z, wouldn't I? Yup, I would.

So all I can say is, that rapper had better appreciate my efforts.

DAY 12: THURSDAY MORNING

So after a whole day riding the rails, we're HERE! We made it to the mouth of the cave. Well, we ALMOST made it.

Mom just spotted some sugarcane growing along a stream, so she told Dad to stop the carts. You know how that went down. But Mom actually WON this time.

So she's out there getting her sugarcane seeds or stalks or whatever, and Dad is tapping his foot so hard, all of our carts are shaking.

I'm excited too, because it looks like a LOT of creeper families are camping in the cave. That means two things:

1. There'll be more creepers to help fight off cave spiders. Maybe those spiders will decide to just take their venom and go home.

2. One of those creeper families MIGHT be roasting some pork chops over a campfire. And THOSE creepers will be MY new best friends.

I really have to stop thinking about pork chops, because my mouth is doing that salivating thing again. And Dad doesn't like it when I spit over the side of the cart.

Okay, so Mom is coming back now. Dad is starting up the cart. (Is he even going to wait for Mom to get inside?!) And our cave adventure is about to begin!

DAY 12: THURSDAY MORNING (CONTINUED)

Okay, so we set up camp. Dad got this fancy new tent that was supposed to "set up itself," but it didn't exactly work that way. In the battle of Creeper versus Tent, Dad took a few hits. I think I even heard him swear (but Mom says I shouldn't write that stuff down).

While I was pretending NOT to write that stuff down, I took a look around the cave. There were tons of creeper families in here, but the best part was what I saw riding a minecart INTO the cave.

I saw SAM.

Well, it wasn't actually Sam, but it was a slime that was every bit as green and jolly as Sam. And I must have really missed my slime friend, because I wanted to jump right on board that cart.

Turns out, the slime was a cave guide named Saul. He offered to take us on a quick tour of the caves, but Dad surprised me by saying NO.

"We've got perfectly good legs," he said. "We're going to HIKE the cave."

Say WAH-HUT?

Chloe grinned at me as if this were the best day of her life.

But then Mom said not to get too excited—that we weren't hiking any time soon, because it was almost morning. "Let's get a good day's sleep first," she said.

So now we're all cozy in Dad's new tent, and I gotta say, it's kind of cool in here. The roof of the tent is like a curved green sky. And I didn't have to climb a vine ladder to get in here.

But it's also kind of crowded. My sleeping bag is WAY too close to Chloe's. And she just warned me to watch out for cave spiders while I sleep.

GREAT. I'd kind of forgotten about them. But now I'm afraid to turn out my torch.

Ziggy Zombie once told me that the average mob swallows seven baby spiders in his lifetime. How is that possible? I asked him. And he said it was because most of us sleep with our mouths open, and baby spiders crawl right in.

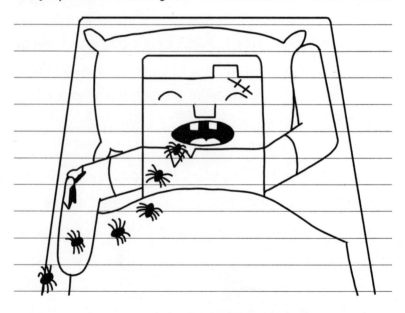

Well I will NOT be sleeping with my mouth open. Thanks to Chloe (and Ziggy Zombie), I probably won't be sleeping AT ALL.

Tent is zipped and mouth is too.
What else can this creeper do?
Cave spiders creepin', crawlin' round
Sneaking in without a sound...ACK!

DAY 13: FRIDAY

Well, I did sleep. At least a little.

I'm pretty sure I didn't swallow any spiders though, because when I woke up, my stomach felt empty. REALLY empty.

When it growled, Mom gave me a carrot. "Crunch it outside," she said. "So you don't wake your baby sister."

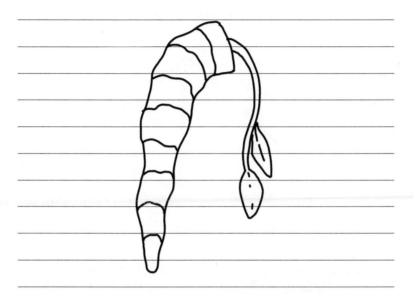

I took my carrot outside, but I didn't exactly CRUNCH it. That carrot had seen way too many days on the road. It was all wilted and rubbery. But I ate it. And Mom promised me we'd find some mushrooms during our hike, and that she'd make some mushroom stew.

Well just the thought of that stew warmed me from the inside out. So, I made LOTS of noise outside the tent, trying to wake up my family so we could get on with this hike already. I kicked a few rocks. I whistled. I might have even stuck my face close to the opening of the tent and hissed.

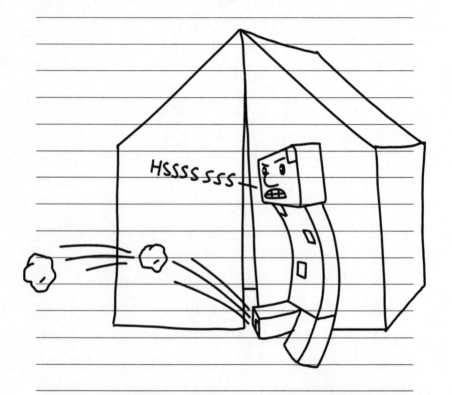

HSSSSSSS

I finally heard Cammy squeal, and Chloe groan. Then the Creeper family started filing out of the tent, one by one.

Cate was the last one out. She was still wearing
her super-dark sunglasses. When I reminded her
that there was no SUN in the cave, she just sort of
sniffed. Then she said I don't know a thing about
fashion.

Then Mom pulled me aside and reminded me that
Cate doesn't have her wig anymore and that Dad
pretty much made her dump out her perfume back in
the jungle. "So leave her alone about the glasses,"
said Mom.

FINE. But I knew Cate was going to be bumping into walls. I just hoped she wouldn't fall off a rocky ledge or into a cave pond, because I for one was NOT going to dive in and fish her out.

Anyway, just as we started out on our hike, I felt the rumble of a minecart coming our way. Saul the Slime showed up and asked again if we wanted a tour. I REALLY hoped Dad would say yes this time.

Mom must have felt the same way, because she smiled super wide at Dad.

But he said no thanks. And after Saul was gone, Dad said that a slime like that would just scare away all the interesting things before we got to see them.

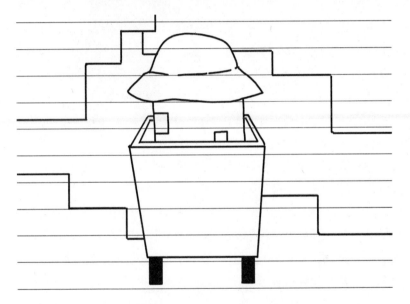

EXACTLY! I wanted to holler. If we'd taken a minecart tour, the cave spiders would have steered clear.

But I didn't say so. After that ocelot incident in the jungle, I didn't want anyone thinking I was a scaredy-creep. So when Dad crept off down a long dark tunnel, I took a deep breath and followed him.

The first "interesting" thing we found was mushrooms. I would have been happy about that, except the mushrooms were MOLDY.

I knew what Mom was going to say before she even said it: "When life hands you moldy mushrooms, make mushroom stew." But I'd been eating rubbery, moldy things for DAYS now. What did a creeper have to do to get a pork chop around here???

I was kind of crabby after that, until Cate walked smack into a wall in front of us. I tried not to laugh, but a creeper can't help grinning. "Told you so," I might have whispered.

When Mom shot me a look, I pretended to be really interested in a crack in the wall. "Say . . ." I hissed. "Are those EMERALDS in there?"

I didn't really think they were. But then Dad ran over all excited, and he pulled his pickaxe out of his backpack, and he started chipping away at the wall.

Suddenly the wall crumbled—I don't even know why. And these disgusting SILVERFISH spilled out!

Well Cammy laughed as if those critters were the greatest things ever. As if she was going to make them her new little pets or playthings. Sometimes I think something is seriously WRONG with that kid.

As Dad dodged a silverfish, he said something that really stuck in my creeper craw. He told Mom that Cammy must take after CHLOE, because she's super brave around critters.

HUH.

Did that mean that Dad thought I WASN'T brave?
I mean, sure, I had just jumped up onto a rock to
get away from a silverfish. But that wasn't being
SCARED. That was being SMART.

Well Chloe puffed right up when she heard Dad's compliment. She started chasing the silverfish to impress Dad even more—or to make me look bad.

By the time all the silverfish scuttled away (GROSS), Mom said we'd seen enough "interesting" things for one night. She said it was time to head back to camp to make mushroom stew.

As Chloe ran past me, she got right in my face and hissed, "Hey, scaredy-creep. If you're scared of silverfish, what are you gonna do when you see a SPIDER?"

She flashed her Evil Twin grin. And then she raced off ahead of everyone else, like she was going to be the first one in line for that stew.

Well that was fine by me. I'd pretty much already lost my appetite.

DAY 14: SATURDAY MORNING

So last night, Mom announced that SHE would be
leading our next family hike. Why? Because some
creeper at camp told her about an abandoned
mineshaft, and Mom thought she might find some
seeds in one of the chests there.

Now normally I would have taken a pass on that hike. See, abandoned mineshafts are DANGEROUS. A creeper could fall to his death in one of those. And it's not only ME I'm worried about. It's Cate in her "fashionable" sunglasses too. Because she's been bumping into walls and tripping over rocks since we got here.

But before I could say all that, Mom dropped another important piece of info. She said we might even find some POTATOES in that mineshaft.

Well, she had me at "PO—" because if there's anything I love almost as much as pork chops, it's potatoes.

"Let's go," I said, leading the way.

Dad was impressed by that, I could tell. But he wasn't very impressed with the map Mom carried. Her new creeper friend had drawn it—the one who had told her about the mine. But it was hard to see the map in the dark.

When Mom grabbed a torch, Dad made some crack about maps being "overrated." Then Mom told him that if he didn't want to follow her map, he could "take a hike"—his OWN hike, that is.

Well that shut him up. But I think Dad kind of DID want to take his own hike. See, he had his pickaxe out, and he was all about finding some emeralds. So I kept my eye on Dad while we hiked, the way I keep my eye on Cammy when I'm afraid she's going to wander off.

Seriously, looking out for my family was stressing me out. My baby sister liked to play with wild critters.

My older sister stumbled around blind as a bat.

And now Dad was playing miner or treasure hunter or something. I had a bad feeling about this hike. A REALLY bad feeling.

When Mom started cheering, I knew she'd found
the mouth of her abandoned mineshaft. So I took
a deep breath and prayed for potatoes. That was
the only thing that was going to make this hike
worthwhile.

The ladder leading into the mine made our TREE
HOUSE ladder seem like a kiddie ride at the creeper
carnival. I slid down that thing with my eyes closed,
hoping I'd hit bottom instead of some sort of trap
door or lava pit or cave pool.

By the time I reached the bottom, Mom was already digging through a treasure chest. "Is that stealing?" I wanted to ask. Were alarm bells going to go off? Were the creeper police going to show up and arrest us any moment now?

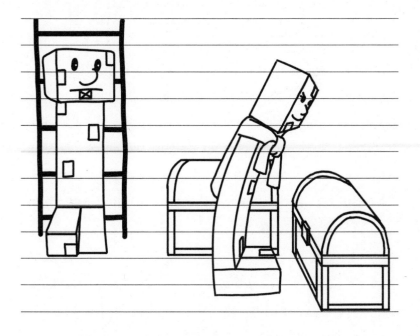

But the mine DID look abandoned. There were cobwebs everywhere, which made me feel better. Until I realized that meant there were probably SPIDERS here too. CRIPES.

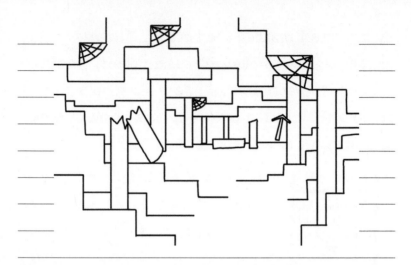

So if I was going to find some potatoes, I had to do it fast. I flung open the lid of the treasure chest next to Mom's and started digging through the "treasures." Moldy bread. Bruised apples. And then . . . YES! Potatoes!

I almost bit into one, but Mom swatted it out of my hand. RUDE.

"That's rotten!" she said. "Can't you smell it?"

Well, yeah, I could smell it. But I had smelled a LOT of stinky things since this vacation started. So I wasn't going to let a bad smell get in the way of my lunch.

Then Mom told me that rotten potatoes were as poisonous as pufferfish. AGAIN with the pufferfish???

I almost cried. Holding that rotten potato was like being near a bucket of water in the hot desert, and not being able to drink a drop of it.

Sometimes Life was SO unfair.

Mom found some melon and pumpkin seeds, which of course were NOT rotten or stinky. So SHE was happy. But then we heard voices coming down the ladder.

I hoped they were creepers, hiking around the cave like us. But when Mom held up her torch, we saw blue jeans. And pickaxes. And headlamps. We saw HUMANS.

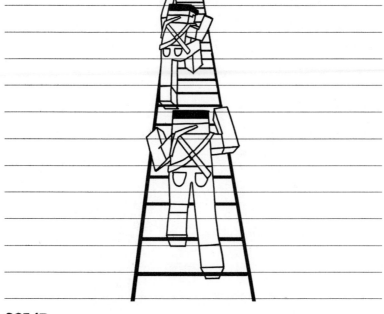

GREAT.

Did we just steal from a mine that was NOT abandoned?

Dad said we should really get a move on, and he pointed AWAY from the ladder, deeper into the mine.

Now I'm just a kid, but even I knew that was a BAD idea. Mom's map wasn't going to help us if we got lost in tunnels down here. But like I said way back when, Dad isn't a big fan of humans. And after the way Mom was treated back in Humanville, she wasn't either.

The only creep in my family who seemed to want to stick around was Cate. When she took off her sunglasses and start batting her eyelashes at the miners, I knew she was in trouble.

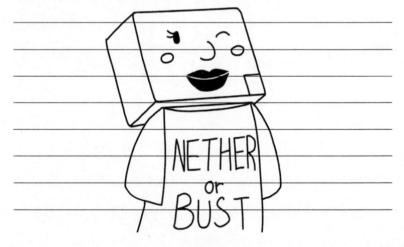

So I did what I had to do. I told Cate that her makeup was smudged. That she REALLY should fix that before meeting the miners. That I was embarrassed to even be seen with her.

Her face crumpled and she put her sunglasses back on so fast, she nearly poked an eye out. Then she crept away before anyone could catch her looking smeared and smudged.

I was pretty proud of myself for that one. Maybe I don't battle ocelots and silverfish, but I DO have genius ideas sometimes. Just saying . . .

Mom had a pretty good idea too. She said if we were going to hike into a crazy maze of tunnels, we should mark our way. So she used a piece of coal to draw an arrow on the wall every time we took a new turn.

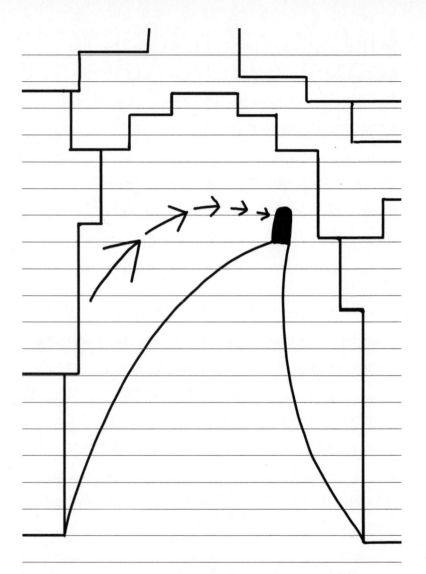

But man, we walked SO far! My legs were starting to cramp up, and I was so hungry, I could have eaten a rotten potato.

Then I heard Dad hollering, and I was SURE the old man had been bitten by a cave spider. I would have run over and saved him, but Chloe beat me to it. And when I heard her laughing, I knew we weren't dealing with cave spiders.

Nope, we were dealing with something WAY different.

Dad had found EMERALDS.

There was a whole wall of glittering green emeralds, and Dad already had his pickaxe out. But when he struck the wall, Mom hollered, "STOP!"

She pointed toward the ceiling. I could see water dripping, but then Mom said it wasn't water—it was LAVA. An orange trickle of it ran down the wall.

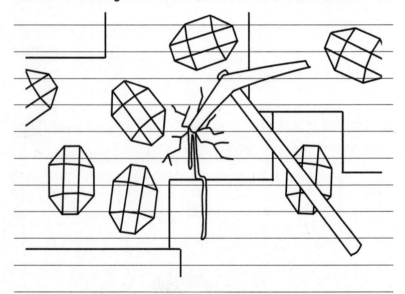

"Saul the Slime said to watch out for that," she reminded Dad. "And not to mine if we heard it!"

But Dad didn't remember. Or maybe he just didn't care about anything Saul the Slime had to say. He raised his pickaxe again, but then he finally lowered it and said something I can't repeat.

I guess for Dad, walking away from emeralds was as hard as me walking away from a sack of rotten potatoes. He didn't say a word the whole hike home. And it was a LONG hike too.

We made it back to camp just before dawn. And then suddenly, Dad was in a good mood again. He started whistling as he unrolled his sleeping bag, and he cracked his usual joke.

So now I'm trying to journal. But Dad is acting REALLY weird.

And I'm way too tired—and hungry—to figure out why.

All I can say is, I hope our next hike leads us to some NOT very rotten potatoes.

DAY 14: SATURDAY NIGHT

So when I woke up tonight, I noticed something right away. I suddenly had more room in the tent. WAY more room.

It wasn't because Chloe had decided to move over and give me space. (AS IF.) And Mom, Cate, and Cammy were still snoozing, too. But there was a big hole where Dad usually slept. And his sleeping bag was rolled up into a ball.

I sat up so fast, I hit my head on the torch dangling from the ceiling of our tent.

"Dad?" I whispered.

Nothing.

Did I mention that Dad is an expert sneaker-offer? He can creep out of a room without anyone seeing him go. It's like he just disappears—drinks a potion of invisibility and vanishes. POOF.

I stuck my head outside the tent and shivered.
Our campfire had died out, and none of the other
creeper families were up yet.

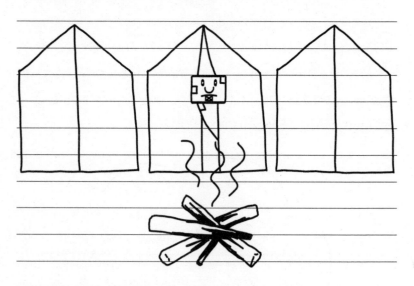

But all of a sudden Chloe was awake. And she caught
on right away to what was going on.

"Where'd he go?" she whispered. "Out hunting for
emeralds?"

As soon as she said it, I knew it was true. Dad had
taken off on his own, which was another VERY bad
idea.

We woke up Mom right away, and she was all like, "I'm sure he just went for a little stroll. He'll be back in time for dinner." Yadi-yadi-ya. Mom could blow smoke all night long, but Chloe and I knew the truth.

While Mom heated up the last of the mushroom stew, I watched for Dad. I could tell Mom was watching for him too, but she wouldn't let on that she was worried.

Then we ate our stew. STILL no Dad.

By midnight, Mom said SHE was going to take a little walk, and that Chloe, Cate, and I needed to babysit Cammy. I watched Mom take off down the railway— probably in search of Saul the Slime. Maybe Dad didn't believe in tour guides, but Mom sure did.

Pretty soon, we heard a rumble on the tracks, and Mom popped out of a tunnel riding in a mine cart behind Saul. She hollered at us that they were going looking for Dad.

When I said I wanted to go too, Mom said NO.
Absolutely not. So how's a creeper supposed to kill
time waiting to find out if his old man fell into a lava
pit or got eaten by cave spiders?

I did what I always do when I'm bored or nervous. I
wrote in my journal. And then I rapped.

Cammy likes my raps. But Cate? Not so much. She
told me to go outside if I was going to be "loud
and obnoxious." Seriously? Some creepers have NO
appreciation for good music. She was probably still
mad at me about the smudged-makeup incident.

But outside, I found Chloe staring at the campfire. I could tell by the look in her eyes that my Evil Twin was scheming. Except this time, she wasn't coming up with a plan to get me in trouble or to make my life miserable. She was coming up with a plan to save DAD. She said that if Dad isn't back by dawn, she's going looking for him.

But as we stared at the fire, Chloe starting getting antsy. She paced back and forth. She hissed. And then she announced that she wasn't going to wait. She was going NOW.

I could have let her go on her own. But then I
remembered what Dad said about Cammy and Chloe
being the brave ones. And if there's EVER a time for
ME to be brave, it's when Dad is in trouble. Right?

Right. (GULP)

So I told Chloe to wait for ten minutes so I could write down our plan. Because if we don't come back from this alive—and I'm just saying IF—someone needs to know where we went and why.

So if you're reading this, Mom, just remember that Gerald Creeper Jr. did a BRAVE thing and crept off into the wild in search of his missing father.

If I don't come home, please tell Sam that Sticky the Squid is his responsibility now.

And if I DO come home, please remember that my favorite meal is roasted pork chops and crispy potatoes. And it would sure taste good after days of wandering around in cave tunnels. Just saying . . .

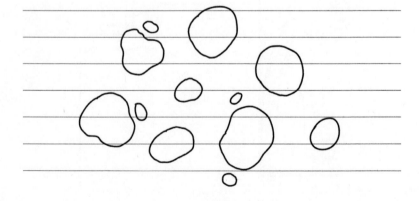

Oh, and in case you're wondering, the wet spots on the previous page are NOT tears. I am NOT crying right now. I was just drooling thinking about crispy potatoes.

HONEST.

Love, Gerald

DAY 15: SUNDAY

You know how two people can remember the SAME night TOTALLY differently?

Well that's what happened to Chloe and me. We had pretty much the worst night of our lives, and she came out smiling and I came out . . . well, NOT smiling.

It started with Chloe telling Cate that we were going for a short walk. And then with us taking off toward that abandoned mineshaft, even though I TOLD Chloe we shouldn't go back there.

We somehow found the path through the tunnels that Mom had marked with coal. But when we found that room of emeralds, Dad wasn't there. And the lava trickle running down the wall was a lava STREAM now.

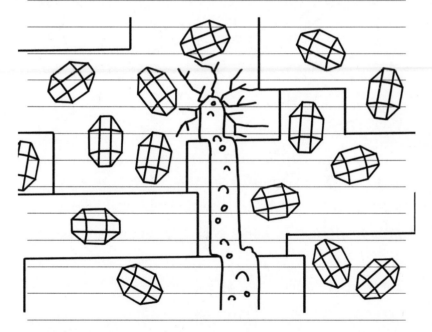

I told Chloe we had to leave that room FAST. Then I saw the giant cobweb stretched across the doorway.

Chloe had already run straight through it, but when I tried to follow her, I got stuck!

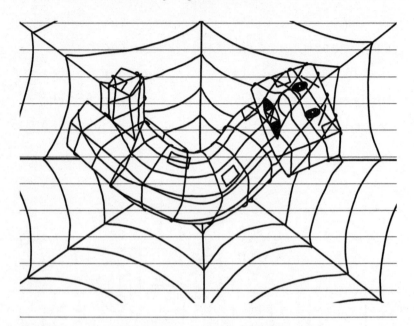

That's right. STUCK. In a cobweb. Woven by a giant cave spider. With glowing red eyes. Who was probably going to come back any second now.

I managed to bust out of that web—with sheer strength, I think. (Chloe says she helped by breaking the web first, but we're gonna have to agree to disagree on that one.)

We ran down a long tunnel, but pretty soon, I KNEW
we were lost. There were no more arrows marked
on walls. And when we ran through the tunnel for a

SECOND time, I told Chloe we were just running in circles now. GREAT.

Instead of coming up with a plan, Chloe just got mad. That girl has NO patience. She said that if we couldn't find our way out, she'd just BLOW her way out.

REALLY? Who in the Overworld thinks that blowing up in a CAVE is a good idea???

My Evil Twin does, I guess.

She blew a hole right through the wall. And then we found ourselves back in one of the tunnels that Mom had marked with an arrow.

So I guess Chloe DID find us a way out. But she also freaked out a whole colony of BATS.

Did I mention I'm not a fan of bats? They started swooping all around me, showing off their fangs.

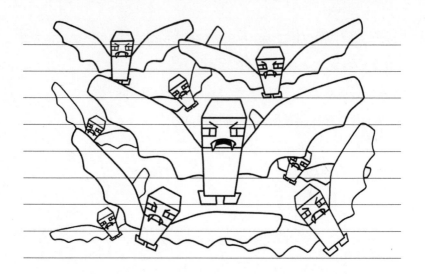

But when I tried to dodge one, I ran into something even scarier.

Another COBWEB.

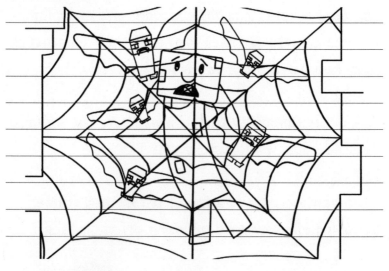

Except this time, I couldn't get out.

Now this next part, I've really been trying to forget. But I think it's important to give you all the facts. I mean, if something DOES happen to me down here in this mine, I want creepers everywhere to know that I, Gerald Creeper Jr., took on a cave spider. And lived to tell about it.

So Chloe must have run off in a different direction. I could hear her, but I couldn't see her. I hollered for her to come get me out of this web, but she took FOREVER to show up.

Meanwhile, I heard the SCARIEST sound I have ever heard in my whole life—even scarier than a growling ocelot who wants my pork chop leftovers.

Yup, you guessed it.

I heard the screech of a SPIDER. (Chloe says that I was the only mob squealing, but I think the girl has some serious memory issues.)

So SOMEHOW I got out of that web, but not before
getting bitten on the foot.

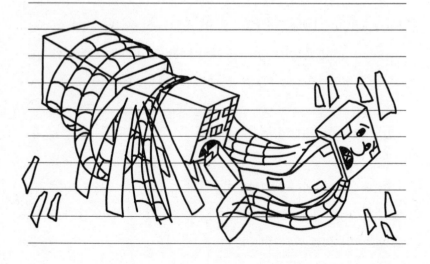

Chloe says I did NOT get bitten—that I just stepped on a sharp rock.

But I saw my whole life pass before my eyes, I swear I did. I saw little Gerald Creeper taking his first steps.

I saw my first day at Mob Middle School, when I met Sam the Slime.

I saw my squid Sticky. I even had the chance to say goodbye to him as that cave spider's venom started running through my veins . . .

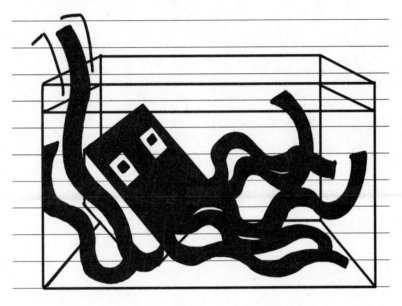

Now everything gets a little fuzzy after that. Chloe tells me she had to carry me out of the tunnel because I was bawling and babbling like a baby creeper. But she'd better not repeat that to ANYONE. A creeper has a reputation to protect, for crying out loud.

So by the time we made it back to camp, I was all set to tell MY version of the story—to tell the whole truth and nothing but the truth, I mean.

But guess what?

There was DAD, sitting outside our tent, eating what smelled an awful lot like crispy potatoes.

Suddenly, my foot didn't hurt at all anymore. I ran toward that campfire so fast, I nearly fell into it.

But there was only a teeny, tiny pile of potatoes left! And when I reached for them, Chloe said that I'd better let HER have them—or she might tell everyone how I was a big crybaby during our hike. SERIOUSLY???

That's when Mom said we both had some explaining to do. "Where did you run off to?" she asked. She kind of grabbed the potatoes, holding them hostage until we spilled our guts.

Chloe and I both started talking at the same time. If I was going to impress Dad with my spider bite, I was going to have to get my story out FAST—before Chloe told hers.

But when we started fighting, Mom shut us right down. "Never mind," she said. "Your dad has some news."

Dad didn't just tell us his news. He SHOWED us. He opened up a sack and poured out a whole pile of EMERALDS. "We're rich!" he announced.

Well finding emeralds IS pretty cool. And finding
potatoes that weren't rotten was almost even cooler.

But how was I supposed to celebrate when the
potatoes were already gone? And when I'd just
had the biggest adventure of my life, and no one
wanted to hear about it? And when Mom said we
were leaving the Extreme Hills tomorrow, because
we'd had enough "extreme" adventures?

When I went to bed this morning, I made a big point
of limping off to the tent. I mean, it would have been
nice if someone had noticed. If someone had asked if
I'd gotten hurt or bitten by a spider or something.

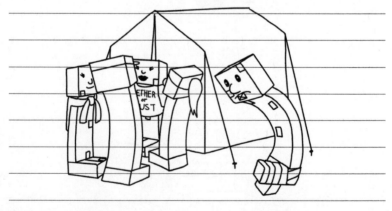

But no one did.

DAY 16: MONDAY

So we're on our way to the desert. I should be excited about that, right? I mean, I'm going to meet my idol, Kid Z, ANY day now.

But for some reason, I'm feeling kind of MEH about the whole thing.

Maybe it's because everyone else in my family has had some big, brave adventure. I mean, Cammy tamed an ocelot. Chloe battled silverfish. Mom climbed jungle trees to get cocoa beans. And DAD found emeralds, for crying out loud!

I THOUGHT I'd had a big adventure with the cave spider. But Chloe still says I never actually got bitten. Now that I think about it, if I'd been bitten by a spider, I'd probably be dead.

Gerald
Creeper Jr.

Valiant Cave
Spider Warrior

So . . . maybe I did just step on a sharp rock.

Cate's not having the greatest vacation either. It's getting hot outside, and her makeup is starting to melt. She has these green and black rivers running down her face, but I'm not going to be the creep to point that out.

Nope, I'm going to keep my head down and pretend like I don't see anything, just like Mom is pretending she doesn't see me writing in my journal while riding in a moving cart. I guess after everything we've been through, me throwing up by the side of the rails is the LEAST of Mom's worries.

DAY 17: TUESDAY

So you'll NEVER believe what just happened.

WE RAN OUT OF COAL.

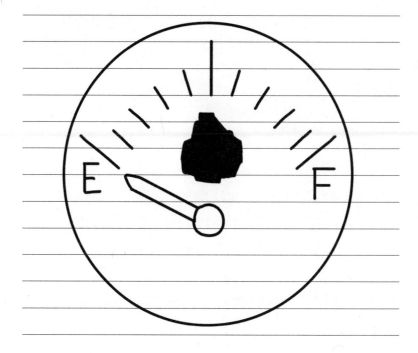

Yup, the furnace cart just sputtered to a stop.
I guess Dad forgot to stop for coal as we were
leaving the Extreme Hills. So now Mom is mad at
Dad, and Dad is mad at . . . the furnace cart.

When Mom finally stopped hissing, she said that Dad isn't really MAD. He's just worried. Because we're on the edge of the desert now, with no coal, so who knows when we'll get the cart going again?

REALLY Mom? Was that supposed to make me feel BETTER?

Now I'M worried too. I mean, what if we starve out here? Or run out of water? Or have to walk into the desert and get lost? SHEESH. This family vacation is turning into a DAYMARE.

And for the record, if anyone is reading this, the wet spot right here is NOT a tear. It's a drop of sweat. Because it's really hot out here. And if we're going to be stranded in the middle of nowhere and DYING of heat, we might as well have gone to the Nether. Just saying . . .

DAY 18: WEDNESDAY

Dear Sam,

If you're reading this, then you know your best friend Gerald Creeper Jr. is gone. I tried to make it, Sam. I really did. I used the last of my strength to write this note to you.

Don't mourn for me. Move on with your life and find a new best friend. You deserve that. (Just not Ziggy Zombie, though, okay? I mean, have some self-respect.)

Oh, and please take good care of Sticky. Put a picture of me near his aquarium so he remembers his good buddy Gerald. Tell him that he was a good squid and that he was loved.

And if you ever meet Kid Z, tell him that I tried to visit him in Sandstone. Share some of my rap songs with him. (But tell him that if he ever wants to perform one of them, he'll have to pay my estate a few emeralds. That's only fair, right?)

Well, I must go now, Sam—toward the light. I think I see Great-Grandma Creeper waiting there for me in the great beyond.

Wait, hold on a sec. That's NOT Great-Grandma
Creeper. I think it's a . . . Could it be a . . . Is that a
LLAMA???

DAY 19: THURSDAY

Yup, that was a llama alright. A whole herd of them in fact.

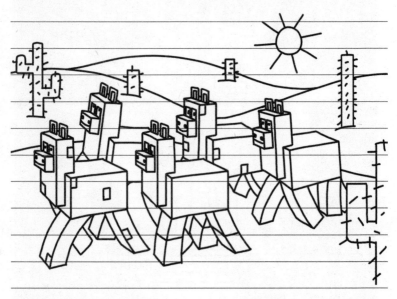

I thought my mind was playing tricks on me at first, I really did. But I guess llamas are pretty common out here in the desert. It's how mobs get around the sand dunes (especially mobs who have just run out of coal).

So when a spider jockey rode up leading a herd of llamas, Dad was more than happy to start loading our luggage onto a llama's back.

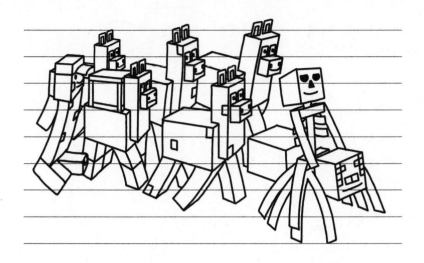

But me? Not so much.

First of all, I'm not a fan of spider jockeys. This skeleton was riding a ginormous spider, which gave me flashbacks of my cave spider incident.

Also, I'm not really a llama rider. How do I know that, you ask? Well, I don't. But I tried riding pigs once, and I know how THAT turned out. (I don't even want to talk about it. In fact, I'm kind of sorry I even brought it up.)

Anyway, I told Dad I wasn't big on this llama-riding
deal. And you know what he said to me?

He said, "We're not stopping."

He wasn't singing "99 Bottles of Potion" on the wall anymore, but Dad was STILL bound and determined to finish this family vacation.

So I got on a llama. What choice did I have? But my llama must not have appreciated Dad's attitude any more than I did, because you know what happened next? He SPIT in Dad's face.

I thought Dad was going to lose his gunpowder, but he didn't. He just wiped his face, took a deep breath, and said to my llama, "We're NOT stopping. I mean it."

Then Dad got on his own llama, and before you know it, we were all heading across the desert toward Sandstone. All I could see for miles around were sand dunes and dead bushes. It started to creep me out a little, I'm not gonna lie.

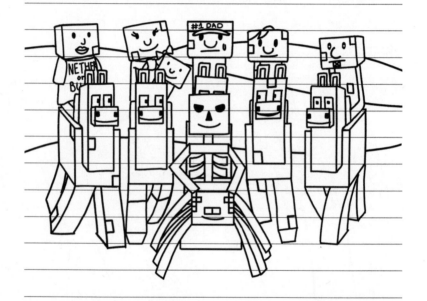

But I kept thinking about Kid Z. I'd do ANYTHING to meet that rapper. And I gotta say, it WOULD be kind of cool to show up at his door riding a llama.

But you know what's NOT cool? Camping out in the desert.

When our spider jockey guide said we had to stop
and pitch a tent, Dad was all like, "We're NOT
stopping." But our guide said it was almost dawn,
and that he would burn up in the sun. (I guess he
has sensitive skin like I do. Did I mention that heat
makes me itch?)

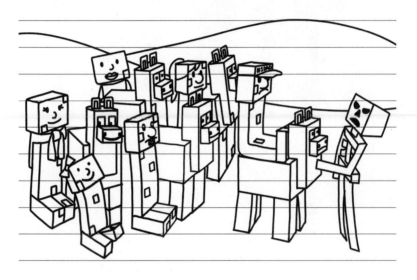

Dad couldn't really argue with that one. So now I'm
sitting in a SCORCHING hot tent in a sleeping bag
filled with sand, trying not to itch. I'm also trying to
ignore Mom, who is right outside our tent collecting
cactus clippings. Is she REALLY going to bring those
poky plants home to our garden?

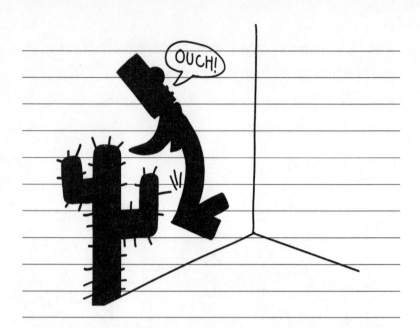

Dad is lying beside me, trying to ignore the llama that's staring at him through the door of the tent. For some reason, my llama REALLY has it out for Dad!

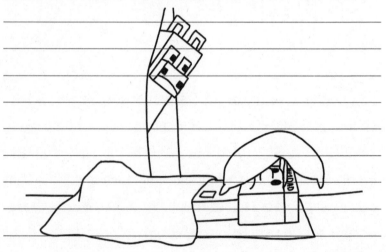

Cate is trying to ignore us ALL, maybe because she's so sweaty that she's nearly makeup free now. No wig. No perfume. No sunglasses. No makeup. No nothing.

And Chloe? Well, I thought she was asleep. But I just found a cactus pricker on my pillow, so I guess Chloe's still awake, pulling her dumb pranks.

Cammy is the only one who is sleeping. Maybe she's dreaming about that desert temple hotel in Sandstone that Dad keeps raving about. By tonight, he promises, we'll have a real roof over our heads. And a hot meal—MAYBE even roasted pork chops.

Yup, by tonight, Dad says, we ARE stopping.

And I can hardly wait.

DAY 20: FRIDAY MORNING

I guess every vacation has its low point.

I THOUGHT we'd hit ours when a hungry ocelot trapped us in our tree house. Or when a cave spider bit my foot. Or when our minecart ran out of coal. But nope, those were GREAT memories compared to what happened last night.

Everything started out okay. Our llamas were trotting full speed ahead, and Dad was determined to get to Sandstone before dawn. "We're NOT stopping!" he kept saying—every time Mom wanted to clip more cactus. Or when mopey Cate fell too far behind. Or when Chloe flung sand at me and made me itch so bad, I nearly slid off my llama.

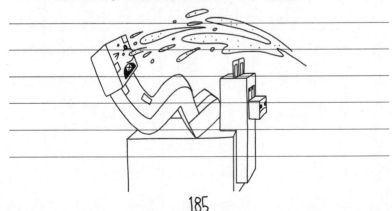

Nope, we weren't stopping until we made it to the temple. And finally, we DID.

The Golden Rabbit hotel rose before us like a beacon. It was almost midnight, and I could hardly wait to get inside. And to order up a REAL breakfast.

But guess what?

The temple was FULL. I could see the "No Vacancy" sign from a few yards away.

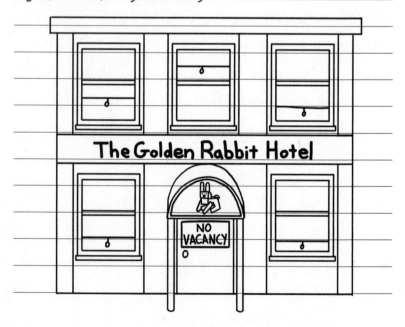

Dad saw it too and *practically leaped off his llama.*
He stormed inside the temple, and we could hear
him arguing with the mob at the front desk.

When Dad came back out, he was hissing mad. I tried
to make mushroom stew out of mushrooms—I mean,
make the best of the situation. I was all like, "Dad,
we can still eat a delicious breakfast at the Golden
Rabbit restaurant, right?"

But Dad said _he wasn't_ going to give a SINGLE emerald to a place that messed up our reservation.

REALLY???

Dad was so mad that Mom didn't even argue when he got back on his llama. He asked our guide to take us to another hotel, a BETTER hotel.

But as we rode on through the night, those "No Vacancy" signs blinked from miles away. I guess mobs were visiting from across the Overworld to attend a Cactus Convention or something.

Anyway, guess what? Dawn is about to break, and we're pitching a tent.

AGAIN.

If I weren't so hot and sweaty and ITCHY, I might remember how hungry I was.

Feeling hot and IT-CHY
Doing this for Kid Z
Dude had better MEET me
Before I starve. . .

DAY 20: FRIDAY NIGHT

Dad and I woke up tonight on the same page. That's when two creepers have the SAME goal. Dad says we need to meet Kid Z and then get out of town. He's had enough of the desert, and I gotta say, I have too.

So we were going to ask our spider jockey guide to lead us to Kid Z's. First thing. After dinner, of course.

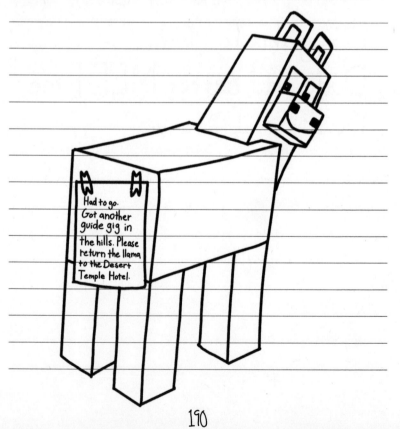

Had to go. Got another guide gig in the hills. Please return the llama to the Desert Temple Hotel.

But our guide was GONE. He was nice enough to leave us a note. And a llama—MY llama.

Now how is a family of creepers supposed to get around town on ONE llama? Dad asked the same question. He hollered it, actually. And my llama answered him by spitting in his eye.

So our night is off to a GREAT start, let me tell you.

Mom says that when Dad calms down, we'll figure out a plan. I told her that maybe Dad was just HANGRY, so Mom should figure out a plan for DINNER.

She didn't really appreciate that comment. She just tossed me a rubbery carrot. So like I said, GREAT night. Can't wait to see what happens next.

DAY 21: SATURDAY

So I have this subscription to Mob Rap magazine.
Kid Z is almost always on the cover. And when I flip
through the pages, I see him on like every other
page. He's EVERYWHERE!

But for a mob who's all over magazines, that creep
is almost IMPOSSIBLE to find in person. I know this,
because we've been looking all night.

We took turns riding the llama all over Sandstone. Well, Dad said he wouldn't ride that spitball of a critter if it were the last ride out of town. But the rest of us rode. And we went from door to door in this desert village. Everyone KNEW Kid Z, but no one knew exactly where he lives.

I'm starting to think Kid Z is a figment of my imagination. Like, I'm so hungry that my mind is playing tricks on me. Maybe my favorite rapper doesn't even exist. Maybe I just made the whole thing up, and my family is going to die out here in the desert looking for this guy.

I _must_ have said all _that out loud_, because Mom suddenly steered the llama toward the Golden Rabbit restaurant—the one inside the temple that lost our reservation. Dad said _he_ would never set foot in this restaurant, but it turns out it's the only one in town. So mom said ENOUGH. She said we all had to eat a decent meal and sort this thing out.

We were waiting for our food to get to the table— the longest wait EVER, because I could smell my roasted pork chops all the way from the kitchen. And that's when Mom made an announcement.

She said _she thought_ it was time to go home.

Well, Chloe cheered. She didn't hold back. I knew my Evil Twin wasn't a fan of Kid Z. But when Cammy cheered along with her, I kind of took that personally.

Cate didn't say ANYTHING. I guess speaking takes too much effort when you're trying to be dramatic and depressed.

So all the girls in my family wanted to go home. But I knew DAD would be on my side. Good old Dad wouldn't let me down.

Except . . . he DID!

He cleared his throat the way a creeper dad does when he's about to deliver bad news. And he said, "Son, I think this vacation has run its course."

RUN its COURSE? I don't even know what that means. I guess it means I'm not going to meet Kid Z.

So now I'm scribbling all this in my journal, and I'm trying not to look at my family. I won't talk to them—EVER again. I'm going on a hunger strike too.

If they think Cate knows how to mope through a vacation, they haven't seen ANYTHING yet. I'll show my family how much they let me down. I'll—

Never mind. Chops just arrived.

So . . . I've decided that I AM going to eat them. But I am NOT going to enjoy them.

DAY 22: SUNDAY

Remember when I thought that sleeping in a tent instead of a temple was the low point of our vacation?

BOY was I wrong.

No, the low point definitely came while we were sitting at the Golden Rabbit last night. My pork chops had just shown up, and you know how much I LOVE chops. I mean, I'd been dreaming about them ever since we left home three weeks ago.

But I realized right away that these were NOT pork chops. I mean, they were chops alright. But after one sniff, I knew they weren't PORK.

So what were they?

Well, did I mention that every server in the Golden Rabbit was a zombie? And that the cooks in the back kitchen were zombies too?

So, yeah. I suddenly realized that I wasn't about to eat a pork chop. I was about to eat a ROTTEN FLESH chop.

Well I started gagging right then and there. Mom got up in my face and was all sweet and said, "See honey? It's time to stop this Kid Z nonsense and just go home. I'll cook you a BLAH, BLAH, BLAH when we get there."

I didn't hear what she said next because a ROAR came out of my mouth. It was like Dad's voice pouring out, and you know what it said? It said . . .

Mom nearly fell out of her chair, and the whole restaurant went quiet. Normally I'd be pretty embarrassed about that, but it was like some other mob had taken over my body.

What happened next, you can NEVER repeat. I'll deny it, I swear.

I picked up my fork and my knife, I cut a huge chunk of rotten flesh chop, and . . .

I ATE it.

I guess there are some times in life when a creeper has to take a stand.

I was NOT going home without meeting my idol. NOTHING was going to stand in my way—not even ROTTEN FLESH.

Well, I don't remember everything that happened next. But Dad ended up paying for a room at the Golden Rabbit hotel. I guess when the owner of the restaurant saw my meltdown, a room magically opened up.

So now the sun is coming up, and I'm about to crawl into a real bed. And somehow, when I wake up tonight, I'm going to FIND Kid Z. Even if I have to do it all by myself.

DAY 24: TUESDAY

I've heard that rotten flesh poisons you before it actually fills you up. Well that must be true, because I slept for TWO days after eating that rotten flesh chop.

When I woke up, all of my sisters were crowded around my bed. Even Chloe looked happy to see me with my eyes open.

And Dad had a surprise for me. He handed me a rolled-up piece of paper. Turns out, the creep who

NEVER asks for directions and doesn't believe in maps went out and found a cartographer while I was sleeping.

Yup, Dad parted with some of his precious emeralds to buy a map of Sandstone. For ME. To make my dream of meeting Kid Z come true!

See this wet spot here? I'll admit it—that's a tear of joy.

Then Dad said something I'll never forget. He said he thought I was BRAVE for eating that rotten flesh chop. "You reminded me that we creepers never quit," he said. "No matter what."

I think the old man got kind of teary-eyed too. Then he asked me if I was ready to meet Kid Z.

<u>READY?</u>

<u>I've been ready for this moment my whole life.</u>

<u>I started to get out of bed, but Mom said "Not so fast, mister. We'll go tomorrow—when you have your strength back."</u>

<u>Waiting is SO hard! But it gives me time to go through all my raps from this trip and find the PERFECT one to show my idol.</u>

<u>It also gives me time to load up on mushroom stew, which is the only dish the Golden Rabbit serves that doesn't have meat in it. And no meat means no rotten flesh.</u>

<u>Yeah, I'm pretty much done with rotten flesh. But you want to know a secret?</u>

<u>It kind of tastes like chicken.</u>

<u>Just saying . . .</u>

DAY 26: THURSDAY

You know what I learned on this vacation? Things
don't always go according to plan.

Like, I planned to show Kid Z my best rap song ever
last night. But you know what I showed him instead? My
dramatic letter to Sam—the one I wrote when I thought
I was going to starve to death in the desert. OOPS.

I blame it on all the bling around Kid Z's neck. I
think it blinded me for a second. I couldn't see. I
couldn't speak. I just opened my journal and shoved
it in his face.

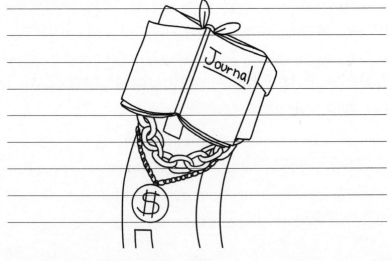

Kid Z was nice about it. He told me that a creep
who writes as much as I do shows real promise. He
actually said that:

So I figure I'll send him a bunch of my rap songs
later, now that I have his address. 452 Cacti Drive
in Sandstone. Yup, we're practically friends now.

My family and I are waiting at the railway for our
ride home, HOME-home. The one where my pet squid
Sticky will be waiting, along with my real bed, and a
real roasted pork chop dinner.

Dad shelled out the big emeralds for high-speed POWERED minecarts this time. "No more shoveling coal for the Creeper family," he said. "No more llamas. It's Redstone all the way, baby!"

Cate actually smiled at that. And when she did, she looked kind of . . . pretty. Maybe it's because she's going all natural now. No wigs or makeup or ANYTHING.

I was in such a good mood, I decided to tell her that. "Cate," I said, "I like your new look."

She thought I was joking at first, but when she realized I was SERIOUS, she smiled again. For real.

Chloe's been kind of smiley lately too. Ever since she saw me eat that rotten-flesh chop, she's been looking at me kind of different. Like she respects me, at least a little.

So I may not be as brave as her and Cammy when it comes to taming ocelots or battling silverfish. But I can be brave in my own way.

And like Dad said, I'm no quitter.

DAY 27: FRIDAY

DAY 28: SATURDAY

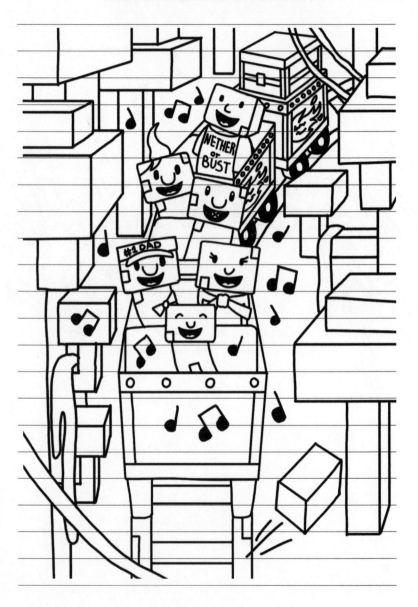

DAY 30: MONDAY

DON'T MISS ANY OF GERALD CREEPER JR.'S HILARIOUS ADVENTURES!

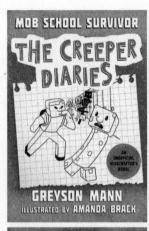

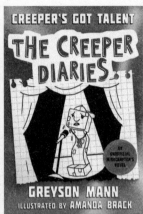

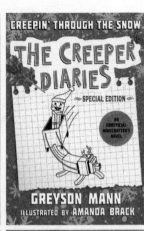

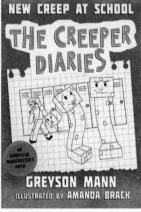

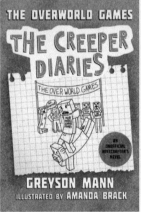

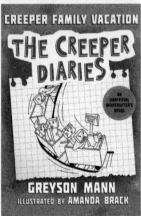

Sky Pony Press
New York